Books should be returned or renewed by the last
date above. Renew by phone **03000 41 31 31** or
online *www.kent.gov.uk/libs*

Libraries Registration & Archives

THE SPECTACULAR REVENGE OF SUZI SIMS

VIVIAN FRENCH

Illustrated by
Julia Patton

For dearest Clairemarie

First published in 2019 in Great Britain by
Barrington Stoke Ltd
18 Walker Street, Edinburgh, EH3 7LP

www.barringtonstoke.co.uk

Text © 2019 Vivian French
Illustrations © 2019 Julia Patton

A CIP catalogue record for this book is available from the British Library upon request

ISBN: 978-1-78112-870-1

Printed in China by Leo

CONTENTS

This is the diary of Suzi Sims,

SUPER-STAR RUNNER —
OLYMPIAN IN TRAINING!

Do not read.

Especially do not read if your name
is Super Sneak Barbie Meek.

This diary is all about YOU!

Monday

Two weeks to go until the end of term, and next week it's Sports Day. I can't wait! I've always dreamed about winning the 100 metres ... and if I did, I'd win the Harrison Primary Sports Medal!

This morning started well. I always run to school, because I love running, and it's great practice for Sports Day. I leave home at twenty past eight, and if I get past the church clock before it strikes half past eight I'm doing really well. Today I was WAY past when it struck, and that was SUCH a great feeling! It was going to be the best Monday ever!

I was so pleased that I dashed round the last corner, and ...

CRASH!

I sent a little old lady's shopping trolley flying, and everything fell out.

Oooops, I thought. I rushed to pick up the cans and bottles, and to say I was sorry, but before I could say anything, the old lady shook her fist in my face.

"You nasty little madam! You did that on purpose! I know you did! I know all about girls like you – all you ever think of is yourselves! Where do you live? I'm going to tell your mother!"

"I'm ever so sorry," I said. "I wasn't looking where I was going ... it was an accident. Honestly, I'm really sorry!"

"It's no good being sorry now." The little old lady scowled at me. "It's too late. You're in trouble! And I asked you where you live!"

I gulped. "27 Laurel Gardens."

"Right! I'm going round there right now!" She shook her fist one last time and stomped off down the road.

I sighed as I watched her go. My mum wouldn't be in; she works at the local garage every day until four. But what if the old lady came back later? Mum would be very angry with me. I'm always having accidents.

Oh well, I thought, and I hurried off to school.

I was a bit late, but it was OK. I tried to explain that I'd had to stop and talk to an old lady, but my teacher, Mrs Hart, wasn't interested. She kept sneezing and blowing her nose.

"Go and sit down, Suzi," she said. So I did.

Ranjit turned to look at me as I sat down next to him.

"Bumped into someone?" he asked.

I nodded, and Ranjit grinned at me. "Suzi the human cannonball strikes again!"

That cheered me up. Ranjit always does.
We've been friends for years, and he knows me
really well.

Mrs Hart sneezed and sneezed and
SNEEZED. Ranjit said he counted forty-seven
sneezes before break, but I think it was more.
Mrs Hart didn't come back after lunch, and our
head teacher, Mrs Nair, came to look after our
class. She kept having to rush out to answer
the phone, so she let us read or draw.

I told you it was going to be a good Monday.
Apart from the little old lady, of course.

Tuesday

Today didn't start very well. The old lady had left Mum a very cross note, so breakfast was all about "Being more careful!" and "How many times do I have to tell you to look where you're going?!"

I didn't try to beat the church clock. I half ran, half walked. I decided it was going to be a dull sort of day.

In fact, it was a lot worse than that. Mrs Hart was still away, so we had Mrs Nair again. She gave us some Maths, but she had even more phone calls, so we didn't really do any work. Barbie Meek even started to paint her nails. Barbie's really fussy about the way she looks; she likes to be the best at everything. She hates me because she's good at running … and I am, too.

When Mrs Nair came back, I was standing on a table.

"Suzi!" Mrs Nair was furious. "What on earth are you doing?"

I explained that I was trying to open the window because the smell of Barbie's nail polish made me feel sick.

"What nail polish?" Mrs Nair looked round, but Barbie was bent over her Maths book. All she had on her table was her pencil case.

"Suzi, get down at once." Mrs Nair frowned at me and then at Barbie. "Have you been painting your nails, Barbie?"

Barbie smiled her sweetest smile. "Me, Mrs Nair? I painted them last night. I'd never paint them in school. I know it's not allowed."

Mrs Hart would have known at once that Barbie was lying, but Mrs Nair didn't know her so well. "I'm glad to hear you know the school rules," she said, and then she turned to me. "Why aren't you back in your seat yet, Suzi?"

"Sorry," I said, and I squeezed in between the tables. My elbow caught Barbie's enormous pencil case, and it crashed to the floor ...

and the zip split ...

and two bottles of nail polish fell out ...

Mrs Nair was NOT happy. Barbie was told off big time: once for having nail polish in school and a second time for lying. Mrs Nair kept her in at break and took away her little sparkly bottles.

Once she had finished telling Barbie off, Mrs Nair turned to speak to the whole class. "Now, all of you – please get on with your work. I have to make one more phone call. Poor Mrs Hart won't be back until after Sports Day, so a supply teacher is going to take your lessons until then."

As Mrs Nair hurried out, Barbie spun round to face me, and her green eyes narrowed. She looked like an angry cat. "I'll get you for that, Suzi Sims!" she hissed. "Just you wait!"

"Watch me tremble," I said. "I'm terrified!"

I wasn't exactly terrified, but I did feel a bit anxious. Barbie has her own friends, and she doesn't often take any notice of me ... but now I'd upset her. And an upset Barbie Meek was so mean she made rattlesnakes look like fluffy kittens.

Wednesday

I ran fast this morning, and I beat the church clock, but it didn't make me feel good.

Ranjit was waiting for me in the playground.

"Barbie's just stormed past, and she had a face like thunder," he said. "She was hopping mad yesterday, wasn't she?"

"Yes," I said. "Don't remind me."

Ranjit grinned. "Don't worry about her. What can she do? It's nearly the end of term."

I nodded and hoped he was right ... but when I got into the classroom, the first thing I saw was Barbie's face. If looks could kill, I'd have been flat on the floor with a ruler in my heart and bottles of sparkly nail polish stuffed up my nose.

Uh oh, I thought. *Trouble ahead.*

Mrs Nair came in to take the register.

"I've got some good news," she announced. "I've found a supply teacher! She'll be here after break."

I think we were meant to be pleased, because Mrs Nair waited a moment for us all to smile and cheer, but we didn't.

"Her name's Miss Grit," she said. "Please make her welcome, and, Suzi! Do try not to knock anything over."

Barbie put up her hand. "Mrs Nair ... is she old, with white hair? And blue eyes? And glasses? And a stick?"

Mrs Nair was surprised. "Do you know her, Barbie?"

Barbie looked like a cat that had swallowed an enormous dish of the very best cream. "Oh, yes," she said. "She lived next door to us a long time ago. She's ever so nice."

At break-time, everyone crowded round Barbie. Well, everyone except me and Ranjit. We sort of waited at the edge. I didn't want to get too close.

"What's she really like, this Miss Grit?" Kiki Dodd asked.

"Lovely." Barbie had the smuggest smile. "She used to give me sweets all the time. She said I was her darling girl."

Ranjit nudged me. "If she thinks Barbie's a darling, we've got a rocky ride ahead."

When Mrs Nair brought Miss Grit into the classroom, I nearly fainted.

It was the little old lady. The one who had shouted at me. The one who had written a horrible letter to my mum. When she saw me, her mouth twisted as if she'd just sucked on a very sour lemon ... and she whispered something to Mrs Nair.

Mrs Nair looked shocked, but all she said was, "I'm sorry to say that Suzi often has those sort of accidents. Perhaps you can forgive and forget?"

Miss Grit gave a tinkling laugh, but it sounded really fake. "Oh, of course, Mrs Nair," she said, but her eyes were like cold hard beads.

Mrs Nair didn't notice. After she'd showed Mrs Grit where everything was and we'd all said good morning to her, she left.

As soon as Mrs Nair had gone, Barbie put up her hand. "Hello! Do you remember me, Miss Grit?"

"Goodness me! If it isn't my little Barbie Meek, all grown up!" Miss Grit looked thrilled. "How are you, dear?"

"I'd like to welcome you to Harrison Primary, Miss Grit. I do hope you'll be very happy here." Barbie sounded sweet as honey, and Ranjit made a face.

"Yuck," he whispered. "Pass the sick bucket!"

I almost needed a sick bucket too. There was a chilly feeling in my stomach, as if I'd swallowed an ice lolly in one big gulp. I'd made Barbie hate me ... and now I had a teacher who hated me as well.

"Thank you, Barbie," Miss Grit said. "It's such a nice surprise to see someone I know! In fact, I think I shall make you my special helper. I know what a very lovely girl you are." She dipped into her handbag, brought out a red rosette and pinned it to Barbie's cardigan.

A "special helper"? What did she mean?

Barbie was glowing as Miss Grit patted her arm.

"Now, Barbie dear, do feel free to come and tell me anything you think I need to know." She gave Barbie a little wink. "You know this class so much better than I do. I'd love you to help me!"

"Oh, YES, Miss Grit!" Barbie looked SO pleased. "I'm sure I'll have lots to tell you!"

I knew then what a "special helper" was. It was a spy.

Miss Grit walked up to the whiteboard and picked up a marker pen.

"Now, my dears, let's start as we mean to go on. I have one or two little rules. Hee hee hee!" she laughed, but again it didn't sound as if she meant it.

Barbie whispered, "Isn't she sweet?" just loud enough to be heard, and Miss Grit gave her a big smile and then turned back to the board.

"RULE ONE! NO TALKING IN CLASS!" she wrote. She read it out loud, and then she laughed again. "Silly me! Of course you can talk when I ask you a question. And when I say you can. Hee hee hee! Haw haw haw!"

I wondered if it was only me who thought her laugh sounded fake. Barbie, Kiki and all the rest of Barbie's gang giggled as if Miss Grit had made the best joke ever.

I looked at Ranjit, and he made a face.

"Laughs like a hyena," he whispered.

At once, Miss Grit swung round from the whiteboard. "What was that? Who spoke? Whoever it was, stand up right now!"

"It was Suzi, Miss Grit!" Barbie had her hand up. "Suzi Sims said you laugh like a hyena!"

Ranjit jumped to his feet. "It wasn't Suzi! It was me!"

Miss Grit took no notice of Ranjit. She grabbed my wrist, and her fingers were hard as steel. "I will NOT tolerate cheekiness in my class!" she hissed, and she scowled at me. "I might have known it was you! Go and stand outside until I tell you to come back in!" And she marched me to the door and pushed me out into the corridor.

Wednesday, part two

I'd never been sent out of class before, and I didn't like it one bit.

I pretended I was in the corridor to look at the infants' pictures of wibbly wobbly sandcastles, but it didn't fool anyone. Everyone stared at me as they walked past, and the little ones giggled.

"Ooooh! Look! Suzi Sims has been a naughty girl!"

When Mrs Nair came out of her office to ask why I was there, I didn't know what to say.

I couldn't tell her what Barbie had done, and I'd never ever sneak on Ranjit. In the end, I said I'd been sent out for talking, and Mrs Nair frowned.

"You've let me down, Suzi. Come into my office and write a letter to Miss Grit to say you're sorry."

Sorry? I thought. *Huh!* But I didn't say anything.

I went with Mrs Nair, and she sat me next to her desk and gave me a pen and a piece of paper. "Show me when you've finished," she ordered.

I had to sit in the office until lunch-time.

Mrs Nair took my letter to our classroom, and when she came back she was looking annoyed.

"Miss Grit says you're a trouble-maker, Suzi. I do hope you can settle down. But tell me – did you really knock her over?"

I did my best to explain. Mrs Nair listened to everything I said, and when I'd finished she sighed.

"Just try to be more careful in future. Now, go and have your lunch."

As I walked down the corridor, the bell went, and Ranjit came hurtling out of the classroom.

"Miss Grit's AWFUL!" he said. "She gave us a really difficult Maths test. Kiki marked Barbie's paper, and Barbie marked Kiki's – and guess what?"

It wasn't difficult to guess. "They both got ten out of ten," I said.

Ranjit nodded. "Right. And the rest of us didn't, because we didn't cheat. We've got extra Maths homework as a punishment."

"She told Mrs Nair I was a trouble-maker," I said gloomily.

"You?" Ranjit was astonished. "Did Mrs Nair believe her?"

I shrugged. "I don't know."

"I bet she didn't," Ranjit said. He made a face. "I tried really hard to tell Miss Grit it was me who called her a hyena, but Barbie kept saying it was you, and Kiki backed her up."

"Ha!" I snorted. "Typical."

"Come on." Ranjit headed for the dinner hall. "It's pizza today, and I'm starving."

Thursday

I woke up with a feeling of dread. At first I couldn't think why, and then I remembered. Miss Grit and Barbie.

I didn't run to school. I didn't feel like it. And I was almost late.

Barbie was the first person I saw when I walked into the classroom. She gave me a sly smile.

"Hello, Suzi! You're sitting beside Laura from now on. I've moved your things for you."

"What?" I stared at her.

Her smile grew even bigger. She looked like a greedy crocodile.

"I'm sitting with Ranjit now. I told Miss Grit yesterday how you're always talking to him. We thought a change would be a good idea."

WE thought? Since when had Barbie Meek been in charge of where people sat?

Miss Grit was standing by the whiteboard, and she nodded.

"That's right. I always say that it's best to keep naughty children away from one another."

I didn't say anything. I was so boiling mad I thought I might explode.

I stomped across to where Laura was sitting at the back of the class and flumped down beside her.

Laura's one of Barbie's friends; they always sit together. Barbie's very noisy and Laura's like a mouse, but Ranjit says Barbie likes Laura because Laura's brilliant at Spelling, and Barbie can copy her work. He might be right. When Laura was away, Barbie got one out of twenty for her Spelling test.

Laura looked nervous when I sat down. I think she thought I might bite her, but it was Barbie I wanted to bite. And Miss Grit.

I think Miss Grit was about to tell me off, but luckily Ranjit came charging through the door just then.

"Sorry I'm late," he said, and then he stopped dead. He'd seen Barbie in my seat, fluttering her eyelashes.

"Hello, Ranjit," she said. "I'm sitting next to you now. Isn't that fun?"

Ranjit stared at her. "Why are you in Suzi's place?"

Miss Grit gave her fake laugh. "Hee hee hee! We've put naughty Suzi at the back of the room so she doesn't disturb you."

For a moment Ranjit looked as if he was going to argue, but he didn't. He looked across to where I was sitting and winked. Then he sat down beside Barbie with a long sigh.

"We're going to be bestest friends," Barbie told him.

She tried to pat his arm, but Ranjit moved his chair away. Barbie giggled and patted her hair instead … and then she turned around and gave me a death stare.

I pretended I hadn't seen.

The rest of the morning was horrible. I didn't want to tell Miss Grit, but I couldn't see the whiteboard from the back of the room. I had to guess what she was writing. It was a list of ideas for stories.

Bunny pathways

Mind scrabbling

Sudden feathers

I copied it down. It seemed a bit weird, so I looked to see what Laura had written. She saw me and covered her page with her arm. *Typical*, I thought.

Miss Grit had spotted me trying to read Laura's list. She zoomed towards me like a hungry ferret who'd spotted a baby rabbit. "Cheating, Suzi?" And then she saw what I'd written. "WHAT have you written here? Are you trying to be funny? Because I can tell you, that is not a good idea."

I thought I'd better own up. "I can't see the whiteboard."

Miss Grit snorted. "Don't try to make excuses! You can see perfectly well!"

"No, she can't." Ranjit was standing up, waving his arms. "That's why she doesn't sit at the back."

Miss Grit frowned at him. "When I want your opinion, young man, I'll ask for it."

All the same, she walked back to the whiteboard and didn't say anything else about cheating. She didn't say anything when Ranjit walked over and gave me the list of titles, either.

Laura looked over at me when he did that. "Sorry," she whispered. "I didn't know you couldn't see the board."

I was so surprised she'd spoken to me, it took me a moment to answer. "It's OK," I said. "Don't worry."

She went very pink. "Actually, I couldn't show you because I'd drawn all over my list." She took her arm off her work so that I could see it.

My eyes nearly popped out of my head. There was the list of titles, but each one had a little drawing beside it. The drawings were AMAZING! There was a tiny picture of Miss Grit as well, and it was so good!

"Those are absolutely BRILLIANT!" I said, and I meant it.

Laura looked pleased. She hid the paper again, and I could see why. She'd drawn Miss

Grit looking steely cold and angry. Miss Grit
wouldn't have liked the picture one little bit.

It was just as well Ranjit gave me the list of
titles.

   We weren't meant to write about bunny
pathways, or mind scrabbling, or sudden
feathers.

   The titles were:

Sunny holidays

Time travel

Hidden treasure.

   I decided to write about time travel. I
wished I could time travel away from Miss Grit
and Barbie; I didn't mind where.

I unzipped my pencil case – and I nearly dropped it.

Everything inside was sticky. Someone had filled it with PVA glue, and I knew exactly who that person was. It was the person who had moved my things to Laura's table – Barbie Meek.

"Is something wrong, Suzi?" Miss Grit was frowning at me.

"I can't use my pens," I said. "They're all sticky."

"And how did that happen?" Miss Grit's voice was sharp.

I shook my head. "I don't know."

Miss Grit pointed to the box of pencils on her desk.

"Come and collect a pencil, and be quick about it. I know how girls like you waste time."

As I walked past Barbie and Ranjit's table, Barbie sniggered. "Keeping glue in your pencil case? What a silly Suzi!"

Aha! How did Barbie know it was glue?

I stopped dead. "I didn't say it was glue in my pencil case! Did you put it there?"

Before Barbie could answer, Miss Grit was wagging her finger angrily. "Suzi! How DARE you accuse Barbie? What IS the matter with you?"

She folded her arms and frowned at me over the top of her glasses. "You're a very nasty girl, Suzi Sims. I think you're jealous of Barbie because she's so kind and lovely. If I have to speak to you one more time, you'll be in serious trouble. Very serious trouble indeed! Do you understand me?"

"Yes, Miss Grit," I said.

Friday

When I woke up, I told myself not to let things get me down. It was nearly the weekend, and it was Sports Day next Tuesday. That was my big chance to beat Barbie in the 100 metres and win the Harrison Primary Sports Medal!

I was smiling as I ate my toast. I always tried really hard at PE, and I knew I was getting better. My smile grew even bigger as I imagined zooming past Barbie and bursting through the winning tape. She'd be SO angry.

I left home at twenty-two minutes past, and I ran so fast that I still beat the church clock!

Result!

I marched into our classroom feeling on top of the world.

The feeling didn't last long. I'd got rid of most of the glue in my pencil case, but my school pen was gummed up. It made my writing even worse than usual. Little blobs of glue kept dribbling out, and the ink didn't work properly. My time-travel story was a disaster.

"Really, Suzi! How can I read this disgusting piece of work?" Miss Grit held up my story so the whole class could see it. "I'm shocked. I really am." And then she tore my story in half and dropped the bits into the bin.

"You can write another story for homework," she snapped. "And if you don't do better than this, I shall tell Mrs Nair to keep you in school on Sports Day."

I couldn't see Barbie's face from where I was sitting at the back of the class, but I saw her sit up very tall. *Oh no*, I thought, and I knew exactly what she was thinking. If I wasn't at Sports Day, she'd win every race. She'd love that! She might even win the Harrison Primary Sports Medal ... She'd love that even more.

*

I was nervous for the rest of the day. I was waiting for Barbie to try to get me into trouble, but she didn't. I was really glad when the last bell went and I could go home.

Two days off school!

Hurrah!

Saturday and Sunday

The weekend cheered me up no end. Mum had been given a pay rise at the garage, and she was very cheerful. We went shopping, and she didn't even tell me off when I knocked over a display of boxes in the shoe shop; she just laughed. She bought herself some boots and me a pair of new trainers.

"Perfect for Sports Day," I said as I thanked her.

She smiled at me. "I'm so sorry I can't be there, Suzi. Do you think you might win anything?"

"Yes," I said. "Now I've got new trainers I'll win everything ... maybe."

Monday

I decided not to wear my new trainers until Sports Day. It was raining, and I didn't want them to get spoiled. Just the thought of them made me feel happy.

The rain slowed me down, and the church clock struck half past eight just as I was jogging past.

Doesn't matter, I thought. *It's Sports Day tomorrow, so that'll be a good day. And Mrs Hart will be back soon. I've just got to get through today without getting into trouble!*

I had a near miss in Assembly. Mrs Nair talked to us about Sports Day for ages, and I got bored. I leaned against the climbing bars; I didn't check to see if they were locked in. They weren't, and they gave a terrible screech as they swung round and nearly squished me against the wall.

Miss Grit scowled at me, but Mrs Nair just told me to stand up and pay attention. It was a good thing I did, because Mrs Nair had one more thing to tell us … and it was EXCITING!

The winner of the 100 metres was going to represent Harrison Primary in an inter-schools challenge!

"It's a great honour for our school," Mrs Nair said, "so you must all do your best tomorrow."

I took a deep breath. I really, really, REALLY had to win now.

Our first lesson was meant to be English, but Miss Grit never took any notice of the timetable. She announced that we were going to learn about a famous sports person, and she pointed to Barbie.

"I hear we have an amazing runner right here in our class! Someone who's going to win the 100 metres in a cloud of glory! So we're all going to have a special treat in honour of our Barbie."

Barbie tossed her hair and looked smug. The rest of us slumped at our tables. A "special treat" always meant the same thing. Miss Grit was going to read us a story.

She only ever gave us tests, or made us write stories, or read us a boring book. She never taught us anything interesting. I don't think she knew how.

"I'm going to read to you about a famous runner called Eric Liddell," Miss Grit told us. She took a book out of her bag and began.

I like stories about runners, but Miss Grit read in such a boring voice that I couldn't understand what she was saying. Five minutes after she started, I was day-dreaming and not listening. I don't think anyone else was either.

Laura was busy drawing. After a few minutes, she gave me a little sideways glance and showed me what she was doing.

It was an amazing picture of Barbie, with ridiculously long eyelashes and masses and masses and masses of wavy hair. She was standing on one leg on the top of a hill, and a speech bubble said, "Look at me! Aren't I wonderful?"

It was so funny I laughed out loud ... and Laura looked horrified.

I tried really, really hard to pretend I'd sneezed, but as I pulled my hankie out of my pocket the drawing slid off the table.

Before I could rescue it, Kiki had picked it up. She snorted and showed Maya, and the next thing I knew it was going round the class.

Oh no, I thought. It was as if an icy hand had clutched at my stomach.

It was two minutes before Barbie saw the picture. I was counting.

She shrieked, and Miss Grit jumped up and snatched the drawing. She looked at it, and then she held it up.

"Who did this?" she asked.

There was complete silence.

Laura had her head down. I could see she was pale and trembling, and I felt really sorry for her. She never gets into trouble.

Miss Grit turned to Barbie. "Do you know who could have done such a mean and nasty thing?"

I knew what Barbie was going to say before she said it.

"I don't want to be a horrid sneak, Miss Grit, but I'm sure it was Suzi Sims."

Ranjit jumped up. "No it wasn't! Suzi doesn't draw like that!"

"Ranjit! Sit down this instant!" Miss Grit stomped over to Ranjit's table. "I don't want to hear another word from you! Barbie, dear ... are you sure?"

Barbie looked up at Miss Grit from under her eyelashes. "Quite sure, Miss Grit."

I didn't argue. I knew Miss Grit wouldn't believe me even if I did. She marched me out of the classroom and down the corridor to Mrs Nair's office. She pushed me through the door ... and then her voice changed.

"Oh, Mrs Nair!" she cooed. "I'm so very, very sorry to bother you. I know how busy you are! But I have a problem. Suzi here has been a naughty, naughty girl. I've tried my best to help her, but she just won't listen. I'm afraid I must insist that she miss Sports Day tomorrow." She gave a huge sigh, but I knew she was only pretending to be sorry. "I know she'll be upset, but she has to learn her lesson. Just look at the horrid picture she did of Barbie Meek!"

Mrs Nair took the drawing that Miss Grit was pushing at her and looked at it quickly. "Thank you, Miss Grit," she said. She sounded very calm. "Please leave Suzi with me."

I thought Mrs Nair was going to be absolutely furious, but she wasn't. She looked at me as if she was thinking about something and sat back in her chair. "What's going on, Suzi?"

I shook my head. "I don't know."

Mrs Nair picked up the picture and looked at it again. "I know you didn't do this. You have many talents, but drawing isn't one of them. Are you going to tell me who did do it?"

I opened my mouth, then shut it again as I remembered Laura's white face. "No, Mrs Nair."

Mrs Nair didn't seem surprised. "I thought as much. Now, what are we going to do with you? I have to say that I'm very sad you're giving Miss Grit such a difficult time."

I didn't know what to say, so I didn't say anything.

Mrs Nair folded up the picture and put it in a drawer. "I suggest you do your lessons here in my office today. And tomorrow as well."

I really felt terrible. "So I can't run in the 100 metres?"

Mrs Nair sighed, and it sounded as if she was *really* sorry. "Miss Grit is your form teacher, Suzi, and I have to respect what she decides. Now, I'm going to fetch you some work to do. Sit down at that table, and I'll be back in a minute."

Mrs Nair didn't come back with my work. Ranjit did.

"Why didn't you tell Mrs Nair that Laura did that picture?" he asked as he put my books on the table. "Nobody draws like she does."

I shrugged. "I'm not a tell-tale."

Ranjit shook his head. "Barbie's as pleased as punch. When Mrs Nair told us that you're working in her office today and tomorrow, Barbie and Miss Grit practically gave each other a high five!"

"If I could find a way to show Mrs Nair what Miss Grit's REALLY like," I said softly, "I'm sure she'd be ever so shocked."

"She'd be totally horrified," Ranjit agreed, but he didn't have any ideas.

As Ranjit left, Mrs Nair came back in. "I've asked Miss Grit to pop in at the end of the day to talk to you, Suzi," she said. "Maybe if you tell her how sorry you are, she might change her mind."

I knew she wouldn't, but I said thank you all the same.

The rest of the afternoon felt like about a week. My head hurt, and I had to swallow hard to stop myself crying. When at last the bell went, I tidied up my work and waited to see what was going to happen. Mrs Nair had gone to talk to a parent, so I was all alone in the office.

I was just beginning to think I should go and find Miss Grit when she stormed in the door.

"So, Suzi! I hear you've got something to say to me!"

I took a deep breath. "I'm sorry ..." I began, but she didn't let me finish.

"If you think I'm going to change my mind, you can think again! That drawing was SHOCKING! I've never known anyone do something so mean and nasty!"

Out of the corner of my eye, I saw the office door open a little ... but no one came in. Was it Mrs Nair? Was she listening?

"I'm sorry—" I said again. If it really was Mrs Nair outside the door, I needed to keep Miss Grit talking. I SO needed Mrs Nair to hear what Miss Grit was really like.

"Sorry? SORRY? Sorry's not good enough! Your work is disgusting, and so are you!" Miss Grit was almost spitting at me, she was so angry. She came right up to me, so close I

53

could see the little red veins on her nose. "You know what? I actually feel sorry for your poor mother, having to put up with such a horrid, spoilt daughter—"

"Thank you, Miss Grit. That will be enough." Mrs Nair's voice was as cold as ice.

Miss Grit jumped. "Why, Mrs Nair! I thought you were in the infants' hall!"

"I'm here, and I've been listening."

Mrs Nair was TERRIFYING! I'd never ever heard her speak to anyone like that. "Please leave this room right now."

Miss Grit muttered something under her breath, but she left.

Mrs Nair looked at me. "Dear me, Suzi. I'm so very, very sorry. I had no idea Miss Grit could be so unkind."

"It's OK," I said, but my voice was shaking.

"It's not OK at all." Mrs Nair rubbed her eyes. "I shall have to think about what to do next. But, in the meantime, hurry home. Hurry home – and get your running gear ready for tomorrow!"

Tuesday

The sun was shining when I woke up. I bounced out of bed and stuffed my sports kit and my new trainers into my backpack.

I ran all the way to school, and I was super speedy! I was so far past the church that I didn't even hear the bell strike!

I had to go to our classroom for the register. Miss Grit looked very sour when she saw me.

"I hear that you're allowed to take part in Sports Day after all, Suzi. I have to say that I don't understand why. You need to learn how to behave in school. You'll never amount to anything! You're spoilt and you're a trouble-maker, and I'm happy to say that I'm leaving tomorrow." Then she turned her back on me.

I didn't care. Miss Grit was leaving! Mrs Hart was coming back! I high-fived Ranjit, and we walked out to the sports field together.

The sports field was behind the school. We shared it with a running club, so the track was a really good one. There were changing rooms too.

Barbie was there with her gang when I walked into the girls' changing room. Laura gave me a tiny wave when she thought Barbie wasn't looking, and I smiled at her.

Barbie saw me and looked over at Laura, but Laura's face was a total blank. Barbie looked back at me and sneered. "Think you're so clever, don't you, silly Suzi Sims? But you aren't. You're dumb, and a clumsy clown, and you're ugly. Do you hear me? Ugly. Have you noticed that nobody wants to be your friend, except that stupid gangly boy? And today you're not going to win anything. Nothing!"

She gave an evil cackle ... and I thought, *OH! That's WEIRD! She sounds just like Miss Grit!*

I went to the other end of the changing room and got my running kit and my new trainers out of my backpack. Barbie sneered at me.

"New trainers? Look, everyone! Little Suzi Sims has got shiny new shoes to make her go faster!"

I didn't take any notice of Barbie. I changed into my shorts and running top, and I was just about to put my trainers on when there was a knocking noise.

I looked up and saw Barbie open the changing-room door.

I couldn't see who was outside, but I heard Barbie say, "Yes, Mrs Nair. Of course. I'll call her!"

Then she turned and called, "Suzi! Mrs Nair wants to talk to you!"

I hurried outside. What could Mrs Nair want? I thought she'd be waiting for me outside the changing room, but she wasn't. Then I saw that she was by the start line, talking to some parents. I went over to see her, but when I asked her what she wanted, she looked astonished.

"But I never asked for you, Suzi. You should be getting ready! It's the 100 metres in a moment."

And then I worked out what was going on. Of course! Barbie had sent me out of the changing room on purpose!

What could she be planning? All sorts of ideas went round in my head as I ran back. I burst into the changing room and looked wildly round. Laura gave me a tiny wink and pointed at my new trainers. I rushed to check them ... but to my amazement they seemed OK.

I shook my head.

What was going on?

I glanced across to see if Barbie was looking pleased with herself, but she wasn't. She was madly opening lockers and checking her sports bag over and over again.

"My running shoes!" she wailed. "They've gone!"

"You had them two minutes ago," Kiki told her. "I saw them!"

"I know I did!" Barbie sounded desperate. "What am I going to do?"

The door opened, and Mrs Nair came in. "Everybody ready?" she asked. "You do know we're running the 100 metres first, don't you? While you're still fresh!"

"Mrs Nair!" Barbie was frantic. "My running shoes are missing! I had them a moment ago, and they've vanished!"

Mrs Nair frowned. "Nonsense. They must be here somewhere! Let's have a proper look."

But they weren't. Mrs Nair searched every locker, and every sports bag and backpack ... but there wasn't a sign of the missing shoes.

And that was when I had my idea. Laura had pointed at my trainers when I came back into the changing room. Did that mean that Barbie had done something to them? There was an easy way to find out.

"Mrs Nair," I said, "Barbie can borrow my new trainers. We take the same size, and I've never worn them. I've got my old ones here, and I'm happy to wear those. I'm used to running in them."

Barbie swung round, and her face was a mixture of shock and panic. I knew I was right. She'd been up to something.

Mrs Nair smiled at me. "That's extremely kind of you, Suzi. Barbie, I think that solves the problem."

"NO! I mean, I can't possibly wear Suzi's lovely new trainers." Barbie tried to look as if she was being thoughtful and caring. "Let me wear her old ones! I can't wear the new ones!"

Mrs Nair gave her an odd look. "Is something wrong, Barbie?"

Barbie began to wriggle. "No, Mrs Nair! Not at all, Mrs Nair." She gave a little gasp. "I'll wear the new shoes!"

"Excellent." Mrs Nair held out her hand. "Your trainers, please, Suzi."

I gave them to her, and she watched as Barbie put them on. Barbie stood up and gave her the fakest smile I've ever seen. "Lovely," she croaked. "Very comfortable."

We were halfway round the track when Barbie started limping. By the time I sailed across the winning line, she had stopped altogether. She was sitting at the side of the track, pulling my trainers off as if her feet were on fire.

When Mrs Nair reached her, Barbie was crying her eyes out. "My feet hurt!" she wailed. "I didn't know it would hurt so much! I didn't know!"

Mrs Nair's face was grim. "What did you do, Barbie?"

"It was only a few tiny bits of grit," she wept. "I tucked them right up in the toes ... they were only little tiny bits!"

"And they were meant to hurt Suzi," Mrs Nair said. "Right. Go back to school and get changed. Report to the school office and wait there. I'll phone your parents just as soon as Sports Day is over. You should feel ashamed of yourself, Barbie Meek."

As Barbie trailed away, sobbing and sniffing as she went, I rescued my trainers and thought about what had just happened. Where had Barbie's running shoes gone? I hadn't touched them ... but if they hadn't gone missing, it would have been me that was limping back to school.

"Ahem." There was a little cough behind me. I turned around and saw Laura. She had her coat on over her sports kit, and I didn't know why. It was a hot day – wasn't she boiling?

Laura saw me staring. "Shoes," she said, and patted her coat pockets. "So silly of Barbie. No wonder she couldn't find them."

"WHAT?" She had taken my breath away. "It was YOU? You hid Barbie's running shoes?"

Laura nodded. "Now we're quits. You didn't tell on me, so I owed you. Besides, someone had to teach her a lesson. You're too nice, Suzi, so I thought I'd better help." She grinned at me. "Enjoy your revenge! I will."

As Laura walked away, I shook my head. *People are weird*, I thought. *And surprising.*

I'd like to say that I ended the day by winning the Harrison Primary Sports Medal, but I didn't. Ranjit and I were way in front in the sack race, and I was so happy I decided to cheer – and I tripped over my own feet. Everyone else rushed past us, and we came last.

Did I care?

No.

Why? Because I DID win the 100 metres, and now I'm going to be running in the inter-schools championship! Truly!

And another thing ...

Miss Grit never came back, and Barbie Meek went off to another school. And guess what?

Last week I ran all the way to school in UNDER FIFTEEN MINUTES! And I didn't bump into anyone.

Life is very good.

Our books are tested
for children and young people by
children and young people.

Thanks to everyone who consulted on
a manuscript for their time and effort in
helping us to make our books better
for our readers.